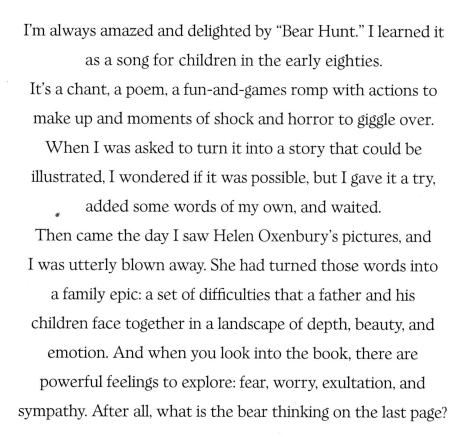

I'm always amazed and delighted by "Bear Hunt." I learned it
as a song for children in the early eighties.
It's a chant, a poem, a fun-and-games romp with actions to
make up and moments of shock and horror to giggle over.
When I was asked to turn it into a story that could be
illustrated, I wondered if it was possible, but I gave it a try,
added some words of my own, and waited.
Then came the day I saw Helen Oxenbury's pictures, and
I was utterly blown away. She had turned those words into
a family epic: a set of difficulties that a father and his
children face together in a landscape of depth, beauty, and
emotion. And when you look into the book, there are
powerful feelings to explore: fear, worry, exultation, and
sympathy. After all, what is the bear thinking on the last page?

Michael Rosen

For Geraldine, Joe,
Naomi,
Eddie, Laura and Isaac
—M. R.

For Amelia
—H. O.

Margaret K. McElderry Books
An imprint of Simon & Schuster Children's Publishing Division
1230 Avenue of the Americas, New York, New York 10020

The text for this book is set in Veronan Light Educational.
Manufactured in China. 0413 WAL
10 9 8 7 6 5 4 3
Library of Congress Cataloging-in-Publication Data
Rosen, Michael, 1946–
We're going on a bear hunt : anniversary edition of a modern classic /
retold by Michael Rosen ; illustrated by Helen Oxenbury.–1st ed.
p. cm.
Summary: Brave bear hunters go through grass, a river, mud, and
other obstacles before the inevitable encounter with the bear forces
a headlong retreat.
ISBN: 978-1-4169-8711-6 (hardcover)
[1. Bears–Fiction. 2. Hunting–Fiction.] I. Oxenbury, Helen, ill.
II. Title. III. Title: We are going on a bear hunt.
PZ7.R71867We 2009
[E]–dc22
2008053214

We're Going on a Bear Hunt

Anniversary Edition of a Modern Classic

Retold by
Michael Rosen

Illustrated by
Helen Oxenbury

Margaret K. McElderry Books
New York London Toronto Sydney

We're going on a bear hunt.

We're going to catch a big one.

What a beautiful day!

We're not scared.

Oh-oh! Grass!

Long, wavy grass.

We can't go over it.

We can't go under it.

Oh, no!

We've got to go through it!

Swishy swashy!
Swishy swashy!
Swishy swashy!

We're going on a bear hunt.

We're going to catch a big one.

What a beautiful day!

We're not scared.

Oh-oh! A river!

A deep, cold river.

We can't go over it.

We can't go under it.

Oh, no!

We've got to go through it!

Splash splosh!
Splash splosh!
Splash splosh!

We're going on a bear hunt.

We're going to catch a big one.

What a beautiful day!

We're not scared.

Oh-oh! Mud!

Thick, oozy mud.

We can't go over it.

We can't go under it.

Oh, no!

We've got to go through it!

Squelch squerch!
Squelch squerch!
Squelch squerch!

We're going on a bear hunt.

We're going to catch a big one.

What a beautiful day!

We're not scared.

Oh-oh! A forest!

A big, dark forest.

We can't go over it.

We can't go under it.

Oh, no!

We've got to go through it!

Stumble trip!
Stumble trip!
Stumble trip!

We're going on a bear hunt.

We're going to catch a big one.

What a beautiful day!

We're not scared.

Oh-oh! A snowstorm!

A swirling, whirling snowstorm.

We can't go over it.

We can't go under it.

Oh, no!

We've got to go through it!

Hoooo woooo!
Hoooo woooo!
Hoooo woooo!

We're going on a bear hunt.

We're going to catch a big one.

What a beautiful day!

We're not scared.

Oh-oh! A cave!

A narrow, gloomy cave.

We can't go over it.

We can't go under it.

Oh, no!

We've got to go through it!

Tiptoe!

Tiptoe!

Tiptoe!

WHAT'S THAT?

One shiny wet nose!

Two big furry ears!

Two big goggly eyes!

IT'S A BEAR!!!!

Quick! Back through the cave! Tiptoe! Tiptoe! Tiptoe!

Back through the snowstorm! Hoooo wooooo! Hoooo wooooo!

Back through the forest! Stumble trip! Stumble trip! Stumble trip!

Back through the mud! Squelch squerch! Squelch squerch!

Back through the river! Splash splosh! Splash splosh! Splash splosh!

Back through the grass! Swishy swashy! Swishy swashy!

Get to our front door.

Open the door.

Up the stairs.

Oh, no!

We forgot to shut the door.

Back downstairs.

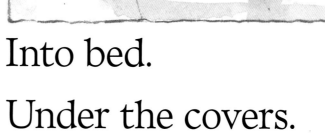

Shut the door.

Back upstairs.

Into the bedroom.

Into bed.

Under the covers.

We're not going on

a bear hunt again.